Ladybird books are widely available, but in case of difficulty may be ordered by post or telephone from:
Ladybird Books – Cash Sales Department Littlegate Road Paignton Devon TQ3 3BE Telephone 01803 554761

A catalogue record for this book is available from the British Library

Published by Ladybird Books Ltd Loughborough Leicestershire UK
LADYBIRD and the device of a Ladybird are trademarks of Ladybird Books Ltd

DISNEY
POCAHONTAS

Ladybird

It was 1607 and the dock alongside the sailing ship, the *Susan Constant,* was buzzing with activity. The ship and her hardy crew of settlers were about to set sail on a dangerous expedition from London to the New World – America.

The sailors hugged their families and bid them tearful farewells. But one crew member, Captain John Smith, stood alone on deck impatient for the voyage to begin.

One of the last people to board was John Ratcliffe, the ruthless and ambitious man who would govern the settlers' colony in the New World. Close behind Ratcliffe was his cheerful manservant, Wiggins, carrying Ratcliffe's spoilt pug dog, Percy.

Soon, the *Susan Constant* was on her way.

On the other side of the ocean, unaware that the *Susan Constant* was heading towards them, a party of Indian warriors were returning home from battle. The medicine man, Kekata, and the rest of the tribe warmly greeted their leader, Chief Powhatan, and the brave young warrior, Kocoum. Chief Powhatan anxiously scanned the welcoming throng for his beloved daughter, Pocahontas.

9

As usual, Pocahontas was off on an adventure with her two companions – Meeko, an inquisitive raccoon, and a protective hummingbird named Flit. As Pocahontas stood high on a cliff top, the wind blew all around her tousling her long, shiny, black hair.

Just then, Pocahontas' best friend, Nakoma, called to her from a canoe in the water below. "Come down here, Pocahontas! Your father is back!" she cried.

Happy and excited, Pocahontas started down the path that led to the waterfall. Then, suddenly, she darted back and leapt from the cliff top, diving gracefully down into the river where Nakoma waited. Meeko tumbled after her with Flit not far behind.

Pocahontas swam smoothly through the water and disappeared under her friend's canoe. With a playful shove she overturned the boat. Laughing, the two girls righted the canoe and climbed in.

"What were you doing up there?" Nakoma asked.

"Thinking about that dream again," replied Pocahontas. "I wish I knew what it meant!"

"Maybe you should ask your father," Nakoma suggested.

"You're right," said Pocahontas. "Let's go!"

13

14

Back at the Indian village, Pocahontas told her father about the dream which had made her feel that something exciting was about to happen.

Chief Powhatan smiled. "Something exciting *is* about to happen," he said. "Kocoum has asked for your hand in marriage."

Pocahontas was shocked. Kocoum was so… *serious*! She certainly couldn't imagine herself married to *him*.

15

"But Father," Pocahontas protested, "I think my dream is pointing me down a different path."

In reply, Chief Powhatan gave his daughter the necklace her mother had worn at her own wedding many years before. As he placed it round Pocahontas' neck he said, "Even the wild mountain stream must some day join the big, steady river."

Later, Pocahontas told Meeko, "He wants me to be as steady as the river. But to me the river isn't steady at all. It's always moving and round each bend there is always something new and exciting."

Deep in thought, Pocahontas went to a special place in the forest – an enchanted glade inhabited by the wise, ancient tree spirit, Grandmother Willow. Pocahontas told the wise spirit about her dream.

"I am running through the forest," she began, "and then, right in front of me, I see an arrow. It spins faster and faster until suddenly it stops! Then I wake up. What does it mean?"

"Well, it seems to me this spinning arrow is pointing you down your path," Grandmother Willow replied.

"But what *is* my path?" Pocahontas wondered. "How will I find it?"

"You must listen with your heart, child," Grandmother Willow told her. "All around you are spirits – in the earth, in the water and in the sky. If you listen to these spirits they will guide you."

Just then, a gentle breeze began to blow. Pocahontas climbed high into Grandmother Willow's branches to hear what the wind might be telling her.

As she looked out across the ocean she could see white clouds in the distance. She clambered out of the tree and climbed onto a rock near the water's edge to get a better view. There, Pocahontas gazed in wonder at the strange 'clouds' – the sails of the *Susan Constant* billowing in the breeze.

21

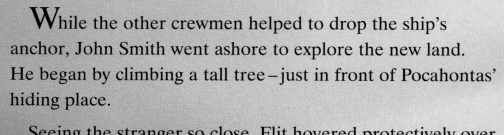

While the other crewmen helped to drop the ship's anchor, John Smith went ashore to explore the new land. He began by climbing a tall tree–just in front of Pocahontas' hiding place.

Seeing the stranger so close, Flit hovered protectively over Pocahontas. But Meeko was not so cautious and scampered over to meet Smith. "Well, you're a strange-looking fellow!" said Smith, as Meeko sniffed the leather pouch where the Captain kept his food. Smith took out a biscuit and gave it to the raccoon. The little creature gobbled it up eagerly.

Suddenly a bugle sounded, calling Smith back to the ship. Pocahontas remained undiscovered–for the time being.

Smith got back to the shore just in time to watch Ratcliffe ceremoniously place a flag in the ground. "I hereby claim this land and all its riches in the name of His Majesty, King James," he declared, pompously.

But secretly, Ratcliffe didn't really care much about King James and national glory. What he *did* care about was the gold he thought he would find in this new land. And determined that the Indians would not stand in his way, he sent Smith out to begin the search for them.

Back at the Indian village, the council were holding an important meeting. Chief Powhatan wanted Kekata to tell him more about the strangers who had landed on their shores.

The medicine man threw a handful of powder into the fire. The smoke that rose from the flames took the shape of strange armoured warriors with weapons spouting fire. Then the shapes changed into hungry wolves.

"Take some men and observe the visitors," Chief Powhatan told Kocoum. "Let us hope they do not intend to stay."

Meanwhile, Smith had walked deeper into the forest and had come across a sparkling waterfall. He sensed that he was not alone – and he was right! Thinking that Smith had gone, Pocahontas had left her hiding place and was walking past the waterfall. Smith, unable to see who was passing him on the opposite side of the cascading water, jumped through the falls with his musket aimed directly at Pocahontas.

The startled pair stared at each other. Smith lowered his musket and held out his hand to the young woman before him.

Pocahontas darted away. "No, wait…" Smith called.

Smith followed Pocahontas as quickly as he could. "I'm not going to hurt you," he said, catching up with her by the river bank just as she was stepping into her canoe.

As Smith held out his hand to her, a breeze swirled around them. Pocahontas remembered what Grandmother Willow had said – to listen with her heart to the spirits all around her. She took the handsome stranger's hand and when they touched, neither wanted to let go.

Back at the settlers' camp, Ratcliffe had ordered his men to begin searching for gold. They chopped down trees, destroying the forest and scarring the earth.

The settlers were being watched by Chief Powhatan's warriors who were hiding in the surrounding forest. When Wiggins threw a juicy drumstick into the bushes, Percy ran after it. He discovered the Indians and yelped in terror, which sent the settlers scurrying for their guns.

In the confrontation that followed, Namontack, a brave warrior, was wounded. Back at the Indian village Chief Powhatan declared, "These white men are dangerous! *No one* is to go near them!"

Back at the river, Pocahontas and Smith were talking and getting to know each other.

Pocahontas taught Smith a few words of her language and showed him the Indian gestures for 'hello' and 'goodbye'.

"Let's stick with 'hello'," said Smith, smiling.

Meanwhile, Meeko searched for food in Smith's pouch. Seeing Smith's shiny compass, Meeko ran off with it and hid it in a nearby tree to play with later.

Smith told Pocahontas about life in London and explained that the settlers planned to build cities just like it in the New World. "There is so much we can teach you," he said. "We've improved the lives of savages all over the world!"

"*Savages!*" exclaimed Pocahontas, glaring at him.

"Oh, not that *you're* a savage," said Smith, feebly.

"Just my people," said Pocahontas.

"Well, what I actually mean," said Smith, struggling to find the right words, "is... *uncivilised*."

"What you mean is, not like *you*," Pocahontas said, coolly.

"To you the land is something dead you can possess," continued Pocahontas. Then, before Smith could protest, she took his hand and led him through the forest.

As they ran through the trees, Pocahontas showed Smith how animals, plants, people—even the wind and the clouds—are alive and connected to one another.

As the leaves floated softly around him, Smith felt her words touch his heart. Suddenly, he was able to see the world as she saw it and his feelings for the land were changed forever.

Drums echoing through the forest ended their magical time together. "I must get back to my village!" Pocahontas said, rushing off before Smith could say a word.

When Smith returned to his camp, he found Ratcliffe in a terrible rage. His men had not found any gold and Ratcliffe was sure that the Indians had it all. But Smith's mind was not on gold. All he could think about was Pocahontas.

While Ratcliffe fumed, the ever-hungry Meeko, who had followed Smith in the hope of more biscuits, sneaked into Ratcliffe's tent in search of food. Percy spotted Meeko and the two dashed into the forest past the wall the men were building to protect the settlement from the Indians.

41

B_y the next morning, the Indian warriors had also put up a wall to protect their village from the settlers. Relations between the two sides were deteriorating.

Later that day, Pocahontas and Nakoma were gathering corn in a field when Smith emerged from the nearby trees.

"I wanted to see you again," Smith whispered to Pocahontas. Nakoma's eyes grew wide with fear. Why was Pocahontas talking to their enemy?

"Please don't say anything," Pocahontas begged her friend as she took Smith's hand and disappeared into the forest.

Soon, the two arrived at the enchanted glade. "To think we came all this way just to dig up the land for gold," Smith said.

"What is gold?" Pocahontas asked. When Smith explained, Pocahontas told him the startling truth: there was plenty of golden corn to eat, but no gold!

Suddenly, they heard a voice in the wind and Grandmother Willow spoke, "Hello, John Smith."

Smith, astonished, stumbled backwards.

"Don't be frightened, young man," said the tree spirit. "My *bark* is worse than my bite!"

Before long, Smith and Grandmother Willow were talking happily and Pocahontas knew that Grandmother Willow approved of her new friend.

All too soon, Smith had to return to his camp, but Pocahontas promised to meet him in the enchanted glade again that very night.

45

When Smith had gone, Pocahontas turned to Grandmother Willow. "I know I shouldn't see him again," she said, "but something inside is telling me it's what I must do."

"Perhaps it's your dream," Grandmother Willow suggested.

"Yes!" exclaimed Pocahontas. "He's the one the spinning arrow was pointing to!"

Grandmother Willow smiled. "It appears you've found your path," she said.

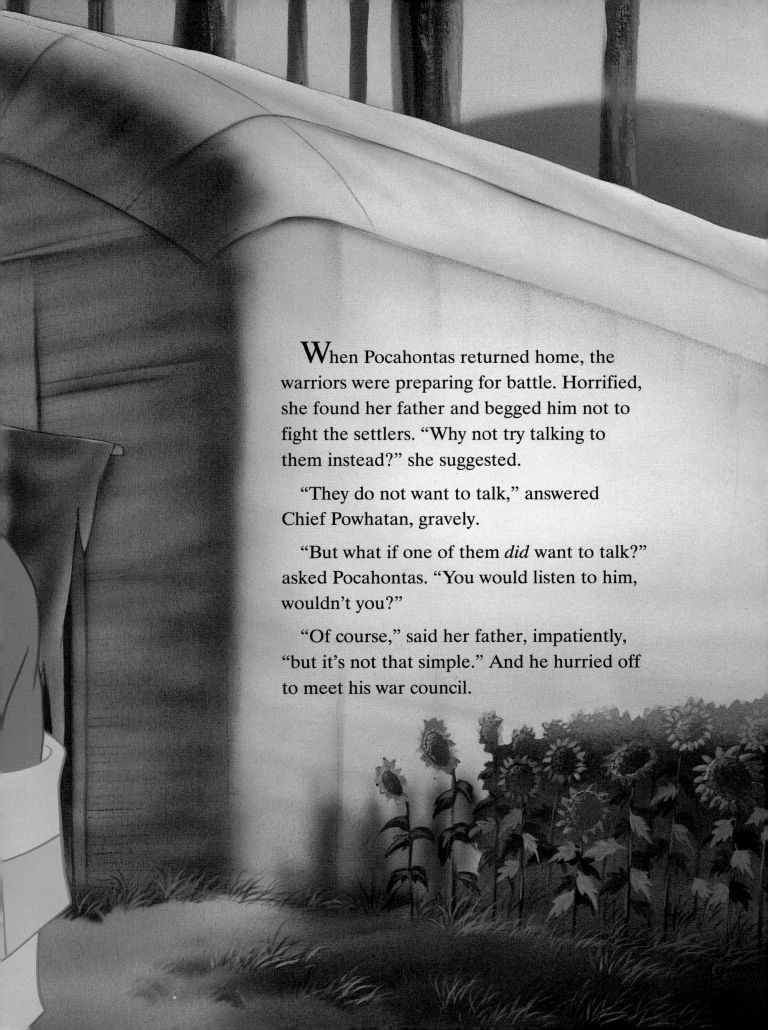

When Pocahontas returned home, the warriors were preparing for battle. Horrified, she found her father and begged him not to fight the settlers. "Why not try talking to them instead?" she suggested.

"They do not want to talk," answered Chief Powhatan, gravely.

"But what if one of them *did* want to talk?" asked Pocahontas. "You would listen to him, wouldn't you?"

"Of course," said her father, impatiently, "but it's not that simple." And he hurried off to meet his war council.

Meanwhile, Ratcliffe was also preparing his men for battle. "We are going to eliminate these savages once and for all!" he cried. "Then the gold will be ours for the taking!"

Smith tried to convince Ratcliffe that there was no gold. "The only gold they have is golden food," he said, showing Ratcliffe an ear of corn. "We can learn so much from them. After all, this is *their* land!"

"This is *my* land!" roared Ratcliffe. "I make the laws! And anyone who so much as looks at an Indian without killing him will be tried for treason and hanged!"

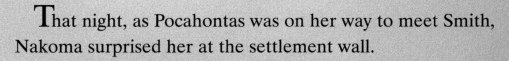

That night, as Pocahontas was on her way to meet Smith, Nakoma surprised her at the settlement wall.

"Don't go to him, Pocahontas!" Nakoma pleaded. "He's one of *them*! You're turning your back on your *own* people."

"I'm trying to help my people," Pocahontas replied, slipping into the forest. She felt sad that her friend did not understand.

Nakoma, worried for her friend's safety, went to Kocoum and told him where Pocahontas had gone. Kocoum decided to follow Pocahontas.

While their people prepared for battle, Smith and Pocahontas met at the enchanted glade. "Maybe it's not too late," said Pocahontas. "Come with me and talk to my father."

"I've already tried talking to my men," said Smith. "It's no use."

Suddenly, Percy and Meeko rushed into the glade. Smith and Pocahontas tried to separate them but the two animals continued to chase each other furiously.

"See?" said Smith, sadly. "Once two sides want to fight nothing can stop them."

Just then, Grandmother Willow dipped a branch into the water. "Look at the ripples," she said. "So small at first, but see how they grow. Someone has to start them."

Smith understood. "All right," he told Pocahontas. "Let's go and talk to your father."

Delighted, Pocahontas threw her arms round Smith and the two shared a tender kiss.

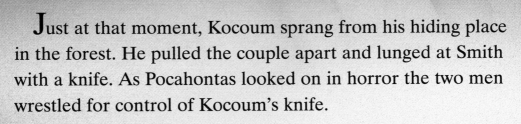

Just at that moment, Kocoum sprang from his hiding place in the forest. He pulled the couple apart and lunged at Smith with a knife. As Pocahontas looked on in horror the two men wrestled for control of Kocoum's knife.

Suddenly, a young settler named Thomas, who had followed Smith, emerged from the bushes. Seeing Kocoum with a knife held above Smith's body Thomas fired his musket, fatally wounding the brave warrior. As Kocoum fell his hand caught on the necklace Pocahontas had been going to wear at their wedding. It tumbled to the ground near his now lifeless body.

"Thomas, get out of here!" yelled Smith as a party of warriors descended on them. Pocahontas watched in disbelief as Smith was dragged away accused of murdering Kocoum.

Back at the Indian village, Chief Powhatan condemned Smith to die at sunrise. When Pocahontas protested, her father's words were harsh. "Because of your foolishness, Kocoum is dead," he told her. "You have shamed your father!"

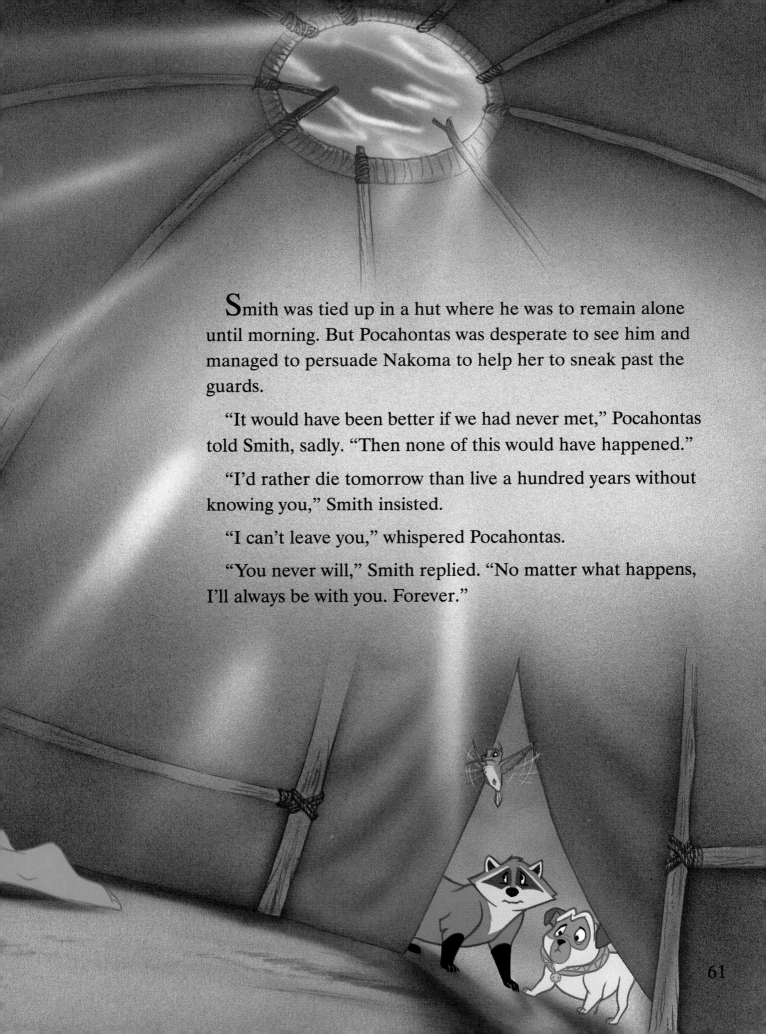

Smith was tied up in a hut where he was to remain alone until morning. But Pocahontas was desperate to see him and managed to persuade Nakoma to help her to sneak past the guards.

"It would have been better if we had never met," Pocahontas told Smith, sadly. "Then none of this would have happened."

"I'd rather die tomorrow than live a hundred years without knowing you," Smith insisted.

"I can't leave you," whispered Pocahontas.

"You never will," Smith replied. "No matter what happens, I'll always be with you. Forever."

Meanwhile, Thomas had raced back to the settlement as fast as his legs would carry him. "The savages!" he shouted as he reached the clearing. "They've captured Smith!"

"You see?" cried Ratcliffe. "Smith tried to befriend the savages and look what has happened to him. I say it's time to kill them all and rescue our courageous comrade!"

Filled with sorrow, Pocahontas went to the enchanted glade. "I thought my dream was leading me to Smith," she told Grandmother Willow. "But I was wrong."

Just then, Meeko handed Smith's compass to Pocahontas. He had retrieved it from its hiding place. As Pocahontas looked at the compass, the arrow began to spin. "Spinning arrow," she gasped. "It's the spinning arrow from my dream! I have to go back before it's too late!"

As the Indians gathered to witness Smith's execution the settlers advanced, ready to fire.

Then, just as Chief Powhatan raised his club over Smith's head, Pocahontas appeared. "No!" she cried, throwing herself over Smith to protect him. "If you kill him, you'll have to kill me too!"

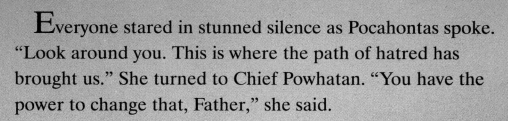

Everyone stared in stunned silence as Pocahontas spoke. "Look around you. This is where the path of hatred has brought us." She turned to Chief Powhatan. "You have the power to change that, Father," she said.

Chief Powhatan listened and heard the wisdom in his daughter's words. "Pocahontas speaks with courage and understanding," he said. "From this day forward there will be no more killing. Let us be guided to a place of peace."

Slowly, the Indian warriors put down their weapons.

67

"Now's our chance, men!" yelled Ratcliffe. "Fire!"

But the settlers, touched by Pocahontas' words, finally saw their Governor's greed and one by one lowered their muskets. In desperation, Ratcliffe grabbed a gun and fired at Chief Powhatan himself.

Seeing what was about to happen, Smith threw himself in front of the Chief and knocked him out of the way. The bullet meant for Chief Powhatan hit Smith instead.

The settlers were enraged. "Get Ratcliffe!" they cried, lunging forward. The Governor was quickly put in chains and led back to the ship.

A few days later, Smith lay on a stretcher as the *Susan Constant* prepared to sail back to England.

Pocahontas knelt by Smith's side. She knew that he had to return to England if he was to survive, but her heart was breaking at the thought of his leaving.

"Here," she said, handing him a small pouch of powder. "It's from the bark of Grandmother Willow. It will help with the pain."

Chief Powhatan approached and placed his cloak over Smith's body as a gesture of friendship. "You are always welcome among our people," he said, softly. "Thank you, my brother."

Just then, Meeko, Flit and Percy came up to Pocahontas carrying her mother's necklace, which they lovingly placed round Pocahontas' neck.

Smith gazed up at Pocahontas. "Come with me back to London," he said.

On the shore, the Indians were sharing food with the settlers. As she watched them Pocahontas knew she must stay and help to forge a bond between the two sides. This was her true path. "I cannot come with you," she said.

"Then I'll stay here with you," Smith told her.

"No, you have to go back," Pocahontas said, softly.

Then Pocahontas watched as Smith was placed in a small boat and rowed towards the *Susan Constant*.

Later, Pocahontas stood on a cliff top as the wind swirled around her. She watched as that same wind caught the sails of the *Susan Constant* and carried Smith out to the open sea.

Though she was sad, Pocahontas knew she and Smith would never be separated. They would live in each other's hearts – forever.